PAVILION

First published in the UK in 2019 by
Pavilion Books Company Limited
43 Great Ormond Street
London, WC1N 3HZ

Text and illustrations © Emma Lazell 2019

The moral rights of the author and illustrator have been asserted

Publisher and Editor: Neil Dunnicliffe
Assistant Editor: Harriet Grylls
Art Director: Anna Lubecka

ISBN: 9781843654292

10 9 8 7 6 5 4 3 2 1

Reproduction by Mission Productions Ltd., Hong Kong
Printed by Toppan Leefung Ltd., China

We were busy searching
in the back yard for
Grandma's missing glasses,

when...

"Grandma look, I've found a cat."

"...Oh aren't you just the cutest, prettiest, most handsome kitty cat," said Grandma.

"...we can't keep you. You must belong to one of the neighbors."

ding-dong

So we went round to ask the neighbors whether they had lost a cat, but...

...they were not cat people,

and, quite frankly, were

fed up of all Grandma's cats pooping on their flower beds and widdling in their garden sheds

Anyway, we kept Big Cat.
He was a bit different
from Grandma's other cats.

Much

more

fun!

Much less grumpy...

...and **much more**

practical!

Grandma couldn't understand why
we kept running out of cat food.

She texted her supplier, Carl-the-cat-food-man, again!

Come to think of it, human food
seemed to be disappearing too!

Then one day the doorbell rang.

Ding Dong

Hmm I wonder who that could be?

It can't be Carl-the-cat-food-man because he came this morning,

and it can't be Grandma's new glasses because they're not due until tomorrow. Let's go downstairs and see.

"Helloooo," growled the callers, "we were in the neighborhood looking for our missing son when we found these glasses. Could they be yours?"

Grandma was delighted to have her glasses back, so she decided to invite the guests in for some tea and cake.

She wondered if there was any way she could help them find their missing son.

"Oh my g✿✿dness!

TIGERS!"

Luckily, **very** friendly tigers.

With impeccable manners.

So now I go to tea with the tigers every week...

...and Grandma has got herself
lots and lots

and lots
of spare specs.

But even with her
new glasses...

...Grandma doesn't notice **everything!**